DISNEY · PIXAR

Merida

The Fire Falls

To Mrs. Haines's fourth-grade class
at Wedgewood —S.B.Q.

randomhousekids.com

ISBN 978-0-7364-3291-7 (hc) — ISBN 978-0-7364-8249-3 (lib. bdg.)

Printed in the United States of America

10 9 8 7 6 5 4 3 2 1

DISNEP · PIXAR

Merida

The Fire Falls

By Sudipta Bardhan-Quallen
Illustrated by Gurihiru

Random House 🏠 New York

There were many wonderful foods in the kingdom of DunBroch, especially in the castle. Mutton pies, fresh salmon, stewed beef—even something as boring as pottage could be delicious on a beautiful spring day.

Merida stabbed her food with a fork. "Why does it have to be *haggis*?"

Across the table, the triplets sat with their arms crossed and mouths closed. They wanted nothing to do with this meal.

"Och, lass," King Fergus whispered to his daughter. "Don't let your mother hear you. You know how she feels about haggis!"

Merida made a show of holding her nose while taking a bite of food. At first her father's face broke into a huge grin. Then the grin disappeared and Fergus straightened up in his seat. The triplets simultaneously uncrossed their arms and picked up their forks.

That's how Merida knew Queen Elinor had walked into the room.

She quickly swallowed her bite of haggis and turned to smile at her mother. "Hello, Mum! Are you hungry?"

Elinor looked up from the list she had been reading and smiled at Merida. "No, thank you, Merida. I've already had two helpings."

The triplets pretended to gag at the thought that anyone would *want* two helpings of sheep's stomach. When Fergus joined in, Elinor caught him and playfully nudged his shoulder.

Merida smiled. Her parents were more than husband and wife—they were also best friends.

They're so lucky, she thought. Ever since Cat had gone back to Cardonagh, Merida had been missing having a friend to laugh with.

"Fergus," Elinor said, "if you've eaten enough, I would welcome your help with the Spring Festival preparations. Can you check the cellar to see if we have enough to drink?"

Fergus didn't need to be asked twice. He practically fell out of his chair on the way to the cellar. Hubert, Harris, and Hamish glared after him with jealousy.

Elinor added, "Boys, would you please go with your father? We shouldn't have *less* to drink after his inspection than we did before."

The boys ran from the room so quickly and gleefully, Merida could have sworn they were will o' the wisps instead of boys.

Elinor sat next to Merida, the only haggis victim left. "Sometimes we all must do things we don't like doing," she said.

Merida sighed and picked up her fork again. Then, to her surprise, Mum pulled the plate away. "I think in this case, though, you could ask Maudie for a different meal."

Merida grinned. "Really, Mum?" She started to push away from the table, but stopped. "Why? You *always* make me eat my haggis!"

Elinor shifted her eyes away. Something else was coming.

"As I said," Elinor said, "sometimes we must do things we don't like to do. Today, eating haggis is not one of them. I need your help today with the final preparations for the Spring Festival. You and I will be the hostesses."

"Mum!" Merida groaned. The Spring Festival was at DunBroch. People came from far and wide to gather for feasting and bonfires. Elinor always handled the arrangements. Merida normally didn't have to help.

"Didn't we just have a big banquet for Cat and Lord Braden?" Merida argued. "Why do we have to have another celebration?" Merida preferred exploring the Highlands with her horse, Angus, to being surrounded by hundreds of near-strangers.

"Merida," Elinor said, reaching for her daughter's hand. "The Spring Festival is important. It is a way to celebrate the coming year and plan for a prosperous future. As the princess, you have a responsibility to our people, to do things that will inspire them to succeed."

Merida muttered, "Sometimes I wish everyone would just disappear."

"Merida!" Elinor's voice was hard and sharp. "You know better than that, lass. The fairies are always about during the festival. They like nothing more than to make mischief for humans. You must be more careful with your words." She sighed, and then her voice softened. "If a fairy were to grant a wish like the one you just made, there would be serious consequences."

Merida lowered her eyes, embarrassed. "I know, Mum. I wasn't thinking."

The queen stood and smiled. "Come along, Merida. Let's go inspect the preparations—and see if we can find some pastries on the way."

Out on the games field, Merida and Elinor were greeted with a flurry of activity. People prepared the areas for the two great bonfires that would be lit at night. Others set up tables for feasting and for trading. Many craftsmen had arrived to sell their wares during the celebration. Everywhere she looked, Merida saw garlands of yellow flowers. The scent of flowers combined with aroma of the cooking banquet food and filled the air.

"Wouldn't it be more helpful for me to stay out of the way?" Merida asked as she accidentally trampled a bouquet. "You know I'm not good at these royal functions, Mum."

Elinor raised an eyebrow. "I have faith in you, lass. I have a feeling you are going to be indispensable during this festival."

Merida sighed.

The job Elinor had chosen for Merida turned out to be arranging centerpieces in the dining area. The queen, on the other hand, focused on the one long table that had been set up on the dais, the raised platform where the king and queen and their special guests would eat.

When Elinor finally called Merida to join her, it seemed to Merida that she'd been arranging flowers for hours. She was happy for the break Mum was offering. She jumped onto the dais, earning her a raised eyebrow from Elinor.

"Do princesses vault onto things?" Elinor whispered.

Before Merida could answer, Fergus said, "This one does!"

That made Merida smile, and she noticed that Mum was smiling, too.

"I suppose our princess does vault," Elinor agreed. She gazed at the horizon. "Are they here yet, Fergus?"

"Any minute now," Fergus answered.

"Who are we waiting for?" Merida asked. She wished it were Cat. But if Cat had been coming all the way from Cardonagh, she would have mentioned it in one of her letters.

"Men from Clan Macintosh are due to arrive," Elinor said, peering into the distance. "And I see them now!"

"Ach," Merida grumbled. A visit from Clan Macintosh meant that Lord Macintosh's son would soon be there. At the Highland Games, Young Macintosh threw a fit every time he didn't get his way. Spoiled and self-centered, he was worse than the triplets—and they were just wee lads!

Within moments, riders wearing the red tartans of Clan Macintosh appeared. Lord Macintosh and his son had intricate designs painted on their bodies with a blue dye called woad so that their soldiers could see them easily in a field of battle. They dismounted and greeted the king and queen warmly.

"Macintosh, you old tumshie!" Fergus bellowed. He clapped Lord Macintosh on the shoulder. "We were afraid the fairies had gotten to you!"

"It is always a pleasure, Queen Elinor," Lord

Macintosh said, kissing her hand. "May I present my son, Young Macintosh?"

"We remember this strapping lad!" Fergus said. "You've grown since the Highland Games!"

Young Macintosh preened like a peacock, tossing his long hair like a stallion tossed its mane.

"King Fergus and Queen Elinor," Lord Macintosh said. His voice was suddenly formal. "My son and heir is here for a very special reason. His birthday falls on the last night of the Spring Festival."

"Tomorrow?" Fergus asked. "Well, congratulations, lad!"

"In honor of his birthday," Lord Macintosh continued, "my son would like permission from to participate in an ancient ritual to prove his worth and loyalty. He wants to climb to the top

of the Crone's Tooth and drink from the Fire Falls, as the brave kings of ancient times have done."

Fergus and Elinor beamed. Murmurs of approval rippled through the crowd. Merida's jaw fell open. She'd already climbed to the top of the Crone's Tooth and drunk from the Fire Falls! Before the Highland Games! Why was it such a big deal *now*?

"Furthermore," Lord Macintosh added, "Young Macintosh will complete another quest. He will find the rare Lady Flower, the traditional gift that the ancient lords brought to their queen, to show their loyalty."

"The Lady Flower is rumored to grow on the rocks behind the Fire Falls. With your permission," Young Macintosh said, bowing, "I will bring you that flower to prove my loyalty, and the continued loyalty of Clan Macintosh to the Kingdom of DunBroch." His tone was formal, like he was trying to be a grown-up instead of the spoiled, tantrum-throwing boy Merida remembered.

"Of course, of course!" Fergus shouted, gleeful at the prospect of a grand adventure. Even Elinor looked flattered by Young Macintosh's plan.

A few steps away, Merida felt jealousy sweeping through her. That great, conceited galoot would be going on an adventure while she was stuck playing hostess. *What good is it to be princess if you miss out on all the fun?*

Chapter 2

Even hours later, it seemed to Merida that every last person in DunBroch was whispering about Young Macintosh's plans.

"Did you hear what the young lord is planning?"

"He's going to climb the Crone's Tooth!"

"But that's impossible!"

"And . . . he will drink from the Fire Falls like the ancient kings!"

Merida ducked into one of the tents, hoping to get some peace. But inside, perched on a table, she spied Young Macintosh—surrounded by a group of girls.

"You're so brave," sighed one.

"And handsome!" added another.

"I just love your hair," said the last. "So soft and flowy!"

"Well," Young Macintosh drawled, "I rinse it weekly with eggs and honey. Keeps it shiny and manageable." He flashed a huge grin.

Merida's head hurt from all the chatter. She tried to leave the tent without anyone noticing. But Young Macintosh saw her and called, "Princess! Were you looking for me?"

"No!" Merida cried. One of the girls giggled. Merida's cheeks grew hot. She stammered, "I c-came in here f-for . . . for this!" She grabbed a garland of yellow flowers and turned on her heel. "Bye, everyone!" she cried, and left the tent as fast as she could.

Outside, Merida took a deep breath. *I need to get away,* she thought. *Just for a little while.*

She walked to the stables to find her horse.

"Look what I brought you," she said, holding up the garland.

Angus whinnied and shook his head.

"Come on, Angus. People say these flowers offer protection from fairies." She stepped closer and stroked his coat. "I wouldn't want a fairy to harm someone I care about."

Angus snorted, then lowered his head.

Merida placed the garland around his neck.

"Let's go for a ride," she said. "I cannot hear one more word about the wonderful Young Macintosh!"

But before Merida mounted her horse, a crowd of rowdy people stumbled into the stable—led by Young Macintosh himself.

"You'll be the first person in ages to climb the Crone's Tooth!" one of the Macintosh men said.

"I bet I'll be the fastest climber in the history of the kingdom!" Young Macintosh drawled.

"You're all wrong," Merida said. But when everyone turned to face her, she blushed.

"Princess Merida," Young Macintosh said, "we didn't see you." He bowed. "I would be interested in hearing what we are wrong about."

Merida felt all eyes on her. She raised her chin and announced, "You won't be the first person in ages to climb the Crone's Tooth. You'll only be the first person since *I* did it."

At first the crowd was silent. Then the laughter began.

"You?" a Clan Macintosh man cackled. "*You* climbed the Crone's Tooth?"

"And drank from the Fire Falls," Merida snapped. The men kept laughing.

"But you're just a girl!" someone snickered.

Merida's hands clenched into fists. She could feel her anger bubbling up. She glared at Young Macintosh and shouted, "How about a challenge, then? You versus me. Right now. Whoever reaches the top of the Crone's Tooth first is the winner."

Young Macintosh signaled for quiet. "Princess Merida, I don't think your parents would want me to let you do something so dangerous." He bowed and turned to leave.

The arrogant galoot! Merida thought.

"Fine!" she said irritably. "I suppose Clan Macintosh is tired of losing to Clan DunBroch."

Young Macintosh reacted exactly the way she thought he would. He swung around. "What did you say?" he asked. His eyes narrowed angrily.

Merida smiled. "I said you must be tired of losing to me. Like at the Highland Games, when I beat you at archery. I suppose you don't want to lose again."

Now it was Young Macintosh's hands that were clenching. "My father wanted me to do this on my birthday," he said. "But I suppose I can do it again tomorrow. So on second thought, Princess Merida, I accept your challenge!"

From the ground, the Crone's Tooth appeared to stretch high into the clouds. Merida and Young Macintosh circled the stone, examining it. At first glance, it looked to be a sheer upright

surface. But Merida knew from climbing it before that the rock was covered in small outcrops that served as footholds.

On one side of the Crone's Tooth—the side Young Macintosh was eyeing—there were many outcrops peppering the rock. But Merida remembered that there was a large section of smooth rock above those outcrops. His way would be easy at first, but soon it would be nearly impossible to climb any higher.

On the other side, there weren't as many obvious footholds. But the ones that were there went all the way to the top. *This is the side I'll climb again,* Merida thought.

Merida's planning was suddenly interrupted by something that sounded like a girl's giggle. *"Hee-hee-hee."* She looked to see if one of fawning girls had tagged along. But she was the only girl in sight.

"Hee-hee-hee." There it was again!

"Did anyone hear that?" Merida called. But the Macintosh men were too busy encouraging Young Macintosh to notice anything else.

Merida scratched her head. There was no one nearby who could be making the sound. Maybe she was just hearing things.

"Princess," Young Macintosh called, "are you ready to begin?" He was poised on the bad side of the Crone's Tooth.

Merida smiled sweetly. "Ready when you are!"

The men sniggered when they saw where Merida had positioned herself. But she ignored them—she knew what she was doing.

At the signal, Merida reached over her head to an outcrop and used it to pull herself up until she found good footing. Slowly and steadily, she made her way toward the summit.

Young Macintosh, on the other hand, was practically flying up the Crone's Tooth. *He is stronger,* Merida thought bitterly. Within moments, he was several meters above Merida. He stopped and looked down at her.

"Princess Merida," he called, "I hope you don't find it rude that I didn't offer assistance to a lady!" The smirk on his face was insufferable.

"I'm doing fine by myself," Merida snapped. Young Macintosh had almost reached the level where there were no more outcroppings or footholds. To reach the summit, he'd have to backtrack down the rock and slide over.

Soon Young Macintosh realized the same thing. "What?" he said. The confusion on his face turned to panic when he realized that he was going to lose time.

Merida grinned and focused on her climb. She wasn't far from the summit.

Beneath her, Young Macintosh huffed and puffed, trying to catch up.

With one final push, Merida hoisted herself to the top of the Fire Falls. While his men looked on, she saluted Young Macintosh and drank from the Fire Falls.

"I told you I could do it!" Merida called down.

This time, there was no sniggering or joking. This time, the Macintosh men cheered. "Merida did it!" they cried. "She won again!"

Chapter 3

To Merida, the bonfires of the Spring Festival had never seemed so merry. Her arms and legs were sore from climbing the Crone's Tooth, but even that couldn't sour her mood.

"Need me to help with anything, Mum?"

Elinor's mouth hung open in shock. "You're . . . volunteering, Merida? Are you feeling feverish?"

"No, Mum," Merida giggled. "I want to help."

Elinor arched an eyebrow. "You're certainly in fine spirits. Maybe you could help your father greet the guests?"

Dad! Merida thought. *I have to tell him what happened at the Crone's Tooth!* She gave her mother a quick hug and left.

Merida found Fergus easily—she followed the sound of his booming laughter. He stood near one of the bonfires, surrounded by people who listened intently as he recounted one of his favorite stories: his first encounter with the demon bear, Mor'du.

"From nowhere, the biggest bear you've ever seen! His hide littered with the weapons of fallen warriors, his face scarred, with one dead eye! I drew my sword, and—"

"*Whooosh!*" Merida interrupted. "One swipe and his sword shattered, then—*chomp!* Dad's leg was clean off! Down the monster's throat it went."

"Aww, that's my favorite part!" Fergus whined. But the laughter from the crowd drowned him out.

"Dad, I've got a new story," Merida said.

Fergus's eyes brightened. "Really, lass?"

"Really!" Merida cried. She pulled him away from the other people and found a quiet spot. "Earlier today, I challenged Young Macintosh to see which of us could climb to the top of the Crone's Tooth first."

Fergus scratched his beard, confused. "Wasn't he planning to climb tomorrow?"

"Yes, yes," Merida said, "but we went today.

With a bunch of Macintosh men who all thought Young Macintosh would win. But he didn't! I beat him! I climbed the Crone's Tooth and drank from the Fire Falls, and Young Macintosh couldn't do either one!"

Merida expected her father to be gleeful. But Fergus frowned. "Aren't you afraid you embarrassed Young Macintosh? Not only did you beat him, but you did so in front of his men."

Merida jaw dropped. "I can't believe you're

taking his side! You're *my* father, not *his*!"

"I'm not taking his side, lass!" Fergus said. "I'm always on your side. You know that. I just don't think it was a very welcoming thing to do to show someone up in front of his friends."

"Was I just supposed to *let* him win?" Merida shook her head. "He guddled it by being arrogant. I beat Young Macintosh fair and square. I didn't do anything wrong!"

Merida turned to go. That's when she realized that she'd been shouting. And that the shouting had attracted a crowd.

And that Young Macintosh was in that crowd, too.

For a moment there was silence. Then someone said, "Young Macintosh was bested by a lass?"

"Maybe he's not as strong and fierce as we thought!" someone else added.

Everyone started to laugh. Even the fawning girls who had been hanging on Young Macintosh's arms pulled away to snicker. Young Macintosh turned bright red under his blue paint.

Fergus tried to quiet the crowd. "That's enough, all of you." But the laughter continued.

Even after Young Macintosh had stormed away.

Fergus finally convinced everyone to watch the caber-tossing competition. Merida was alone— and for the first time, winning felt terrible. She didn't know if she could feel any worse.

Then Lord Macintosh called her name.

"Princess Merida," he hollered, "have you seen my boy?"

Heat rose in Merida's face. She couldn't admit that she'd driven Young Macintosh away by telling everyone she'd beaten him up the Crone's Tooth. So she stammered, "I'll g-go find him."

"Thank you, Princess, you are so kind!" Lord Macintosh flashed a smile.

And then Merida did feel worse.

After walking the glens for a while, Merida finally spotted Young Macintosh. He was leaning against a large upright stone on a bluff overlooking the games field. As Merida got closer, she saw that his eyes were red.

"Hee-hee-hee."

Merida's head snapped around. That giggling again! *What could it be?* she wondered.

Merida didn't want an audience for what she planned to do next—apologize to Young Macintosh. She looked around carefully for eavesdroppers. But just like before, there was no one to be found.

Merida took a deep breath and walked slowly over to the lad. "Hello there," she said. "Your father is looking for you."

Young Macintosh turned. His glaring eyes locked with Merida's. "Why did you come?" he said. "Haven't you humiliated me enough?"

Merida flinched at the anger in his tone.

"There's no one for you to brag to," he added, "so it can't be any fun for you to be here."

Merida exhaled deeply. She'd come to apologize, and she knew he would be upset. "I just wanted to tell you that I'm—"

But that's as far as she got. Young Macintosh stood and pointed to the Crone's Tooth.

"Those were my men watching us today. They need to respect me if I am to lead them. You embarrassed me in front of them. Why would they ever follow someone who can be bested by a girl?"

Merida felt herself getting angry. Why wouldn't he just let her apologize? "Oh, calm down!" she yelled. "You're making a big deal out of nothing."

"Out of nothing?" he sputtered. He pointed to the blue paint on his right arm. "Do you see this, Princess? This woad signifies that I am important in my clan. My father expects me to be a leader. I deserve be respected and listened to. I deserve better than I got today!"

"All this talk of what you deserve," Merida muttered. "You think far too much of yourself."

"Think too much of myself? Have you forgotten who I am?" Young Macintosh shouted. "I am the heir to Clan Macintosh!"

"Forgotten?" Merida answered. "I haven't forgotten. I wish YOU'd forget all this nonsense about who you are! Maybe then you wouldn't be so insufferable!"

At that exact moment, there was a huge clap of thunder. It was so loud and sudden,

Merida almost didn't notice the giggling.

"Hee-hee-hee."

Before Merida could figure out where the giggles had come from, a bolt of lightning struck a tree behind her. She jumped at the sound. In the distance, the tree split in two.

"Young Macintosh," she said, "I think we should get back to Castle DunBroch."

When he didn't answer, Merida turned back to face him. Young Macintosh looked like he was in a daze. He was staring at Merida like he'd never seen her before.

"Young Macintosh," Merida asked, "is everything all right?"

"Who are you?" he said. "And why am I covered in all this blue stuff?"

Chapter
4

"Enough fooling around, Young Macintosh," Merida said. Small raindrops had begun to fall. "It's time to head back to DunBroch."

But he only stared blankly in her direction. "To where?"

"What do you mean, 'to where?'" Merida asked. "To Castle DunBroch, where you and your father are the guests of my parents."

"My father?"

Merida knit her brows. "What is wrong with you? Did you hit your head?"

"I don't think so. I don't remember hitting my head." He frowned. "I don't remember anything."

All of a sudden, Merida remembered Mum's warning from earlier: "The fairies are always about during the festival, and they like nothing more than to make mischief for humans. You must be more careful with your words." She gasped and clapped a hand over her mouth. Merida had wished for Young Macintosh to forget who he was—and right after that, she had heard the strange giggling. *That must have been a fairy*, Merida thought. *What have I done?*

She glanced at Young Macintosh. He was staring at the blue designs on his arms, the ones he was so proud of just a few moments ago. But now he looked puzzled. *If he doesn't know what those are, he really doesn't remember who he is!*

"Young Macintosh," Merida said, "I need to ask you some questions."

He looked up at her. "Are you talking to me?"

Merida bit her lip. "Don't you remember your clan?"

He shook his head.

"What *do* you remember?" she asked, feeling desperate.

Young Macintosh scratched his head. "I don't know." He looked around. "That's a tree," he said, "and we're in a glen." He pointed. "Those are archery targets, and those are bonfires." He turned to face Castle DunBroch. "And that's a castle," he continued, "but I can't remember what castle it is. I don't remember your name. And I definitely don't remember anyone named Young Macintosh."

"Oh, this is bad," Merida mumbled. She began pacing. Then she had an idea. *If a fairy heard my first wish,* she thought, *then maybe...*

"I wish Young Macintosh would remember who he is!" she shouted.

"What did you say?" Young Macintosh said.

Merida shushed him. She wanted to make sure she heard the fairy's giggle.

But there were no sounds other than the soft pitter-patter of raindrops.

Merida's heart sank. What had she done?

She grabbed Young Macintosh's hand and all

but dragged him back to DunBroch.

"Where are you taking me?" he asked.

"Just trust me, please?" she urged.

"Do I normally trust you? Do we know each other?"

Merida bit her lip. "You've known me since we were wee babes." At least that was true. "You came to celebrate the Spring Festival with my family. You are the heir to Clan Macintosh.

We are proud to be hosting you."

"I wish I could remember," Young Macintosh said.

Merida felt so guilty, she had to look away. She had to do something—she just didn't know what. Not yet. She thought of the spell that had turned Elinor into a bear. *That spell could be broken,* she thought. *Maybe this one can, too.*

But first she had to get him home.

By the time they arrived, they were soaked to the bone. Merida spied her parents and Lord Macintosh talking quietly around one of the dying bonfires.

She yanked Young Macintosh forward. Elinor saw them and stood up.

"Merida!" Elinor said. "Young Macintosh! Where were you two hiding?"

"Mum, I have to tell you something." But before she could explain, Lord Macintosh clapped Young Macintosh on the shoulder.

"We were worried, son," he said. "Fergus thought you might have been eaten by a bear!"

Young Macintosh backed away from his father. "I am not your son!" he blurted.

Lord Macintosh looked like someone had slapped him hard, his expression a mix of shock and pain. "What are you saying?" he asked.

"I don't mean any disrespect," Young Macintosh said, "but I've never seen you before. I think a son would remember his father."

Lord Macintosh staggered back. Fergus seized his arm and held him up.

"What happened to you, lad?" Fergus demanded. "This is no way to treat your father!"

Before Young Macintosh could answer, Merida clapped a hand over his mouth and shouted, "He's lost his memory!"

"What do you mean?" Elinor asked.

"I found him out in the glen, and... something happened." Merida gulped. She didn't know how to explain her wish.

Lord Macintosh pulled away from Fergus and placed his hands on his son's arms. "What happened, boy? Did you get hurt?"

Once again, Young Macintosh stepped away from his father. "I don't remember!" he shouted.

Before the situation got more out of hand,

Elinor stepped in. "Everyone is tired. Let us return to the castle and get some rest. Everything will be different in the morning."

"Listen to her," Fergus said to Lord Macintosh. "The lad must have been nutted by something. A few hours of sleep and he should be back to normal."

Elinor turned to Young Macintosh. "Would you return to the castle for the night? I extend you an invitation as Queen of DunBroch."

Young Macintosh looked confused. "I know this is all very strange," Merida whispered to him. "But you trusted me enough to come back here. Castle DunBroch is my home. Please come with us? We can figure out the rest tomorrow."

The lad agreed reluctantly, and everyone headed toward the castle. Young Macintosh stayed close to Merida. "You're the only one here I know at all," he whispered. "I hope you don't mind if I walk with you."

Merida gulped. "Of course not," she answered, forcing herself to smile, though she felt anything but happy.

Inside the castle, Young Macintosh stood in front of Elinor. "Excuse me, my queen," he said. He sounded very formal.

"Yes?" Elinor answered.

"Could I take a bath?" he asked. "I want to wash this blue stuff off."

Lord Macintosh's eyes grew wide. "Blue

stuff?" he snorted. "That is blue woad! It is a tradition of our clan to paint our bodies in blue woad to proclaim we are ready for battle at any moment!"

Young Macintosh shrugged. "I don't remember that. And this blue stuff is itchy. I just want to wash it off."

Before Lord Macintosh could respond, Fergus pulled him away. "Let the lad take a bath, Macintosh. It'll help him sleep. You and I should go to the cellar and have a drink from my private reserve."

Lord Macintosh kept looking over his shoulder as Fergus led him toward the cellar.

"Maudie will draw a bath for you," Elinor said. "It will just take a little time." She glanced at her daughter. "Can I send you down to the kitchens with Merida to get a snack while you wait?"

"Yes, my lady," Young Macintosh answered.

"Wonderful," said Elinor. "Just give me a moment to speak to my daughter first."

Elinor drew Merida aside, just out of Young Macintosh's hearing. "What happened out there, Merida?" she asked. "Do you know why Young Macintosh can't remember who he is?"

Merida gulped. She really didn't want to confess that she had done *exactly* what Mum had warned her not to do—spoken careless words when the fairies were around. But Elinor was staring at her with her most queenly serious look. So Merida took a deep breath.

But before she could say anything, Young Macintosh interrupted. "My lady, should I just find the kitchens myself?"

Elinor sighed, and Merida shrugged. "No, lad," Elinor said, "Merida is ready. Go on, you two."

As they walked away, Merida decided that she would tell Mum everything—as soon as she figured out how to make it right.

In the kitchens, Merida asked Young Macintosh, "What would you like?"

Young Macintosh scratched his head. "I don't know. I don't remember what I like."

Again Merida felt terrible for making that stupid wish.

"Aren't you upset that you can't remember anything?" Merida asked.

"Yes, of course," he admitted. "I want to remember. I'm trying. And I can see flashes of things that I think I remember, but not enough to be sure." He plopped down on a bench. "It's especially frustrating that everyone here seems to know me, but I don't remember anyone."

Merida hated that she was responsible for the whole situation. She turned away and riffled around for some food. Eventually, she found a plate of leftover haggis. "We have this," she said, holding out the plate.

Young Macintosh recoiled from the plate like it was a snake. "What is that?"

"It's haggis. My mother likes it. I thought maybe you'd like it, too."

He shook his head. "I think I finally remember something. I know for sure I don't like haggis!"

The giggle that escaped her mouth surprised even Merida. Soon she was laughing heartily.

"Well, I may not be able to remember my clan," he chuckled, "but some things are too important to be forgotten!"

That night, the castle was as silent as Merida had ever remembered it being. Still, she lay awake in her bed, thinking what a day it had been.

When she challenged Young Macintosh to climb the Crone's Tooth, she knew in her heart that she'd be able to climb faster than him. Just as she knew during the Highland Games that she could beat all the heirs at archery. On that day, she'd needed to embarrass Young Dingwall, Young Macintosh, and Young MacGuffin by winning—having a say in who she would marry was important! Today she had humiliated Young Macintosh over something petty, but she'd felt no remorse because she thought Young Macintosh was a selfish and spoiled.

The truth was that Merida didn't know Young Macintosh at all. Now that he wasn't concerned about his rank or position, she was seeing who he was without the arrogance or ego. She hadn't known how funny he could be. She wondered what else she didn't know about him.

Why did I have to say those stupid words? she thought. *How could I wish for someone to forget his whole identity?*

Merida glanced out her window. Tomorrow, on the last night of the Spring Festival, the moon would be full. It should be a night of celebration. Instead, she didn't know what would happen.

She let herself wallow in misery for a few moments. Then she shook her head and squared her shoulders. "I am Princess Merida of DunBroch," she whispered to herself, "and I climbed the Crone's Tooth and drank from the Fire Falls—not once, but twice. I helped break the spell on Mor'du, and I outsmarted Padraic and saved Cat from his magic. Tomorrow I will find a way to break a fairy spell."

By the time she fell asleep, Merida even believed it.

Chapter
5

On the second morning of the Spring Festival, Merida dashed to the Great Hall to see if anything had changed with Young Macintosh. When she arrived, she found Elinor and Fergus deep in conversation with Lord Macintosh.

"He still doesn't recognize you?" Fergus asked.

Lord Macintosh's fingers clenched the edge of the table. "He doesn't even know his own clan," he grumbled. "He looks at me like I'm a stranger! His own father!"

"Does he remember anything?" asked Elinor.

"Small things," Lord Macintosh said. "He seems to remember his name, but not his title. He doesn't respond to anyone calling for Young Macintosh! And he doesn't remember that today is his birthday!"

"There, there," Elinor soothed. "It will be all right. We will find a way to cure him."

Merida turned away. *I have to do something to fix this. But what?*

"Merida?" Dad's voice surprised her. "Is everything all right, lass?"

Merida didn't know where to begin.

Then Fergus said, "I think I already know what's bothering you."

Merida stared. "What?" she gasped.

"Your mother thinks she has special powers that let her know what her children are thinking," Fergus said. "But I'm your father. I always know what's in your heart." He cupped his daughter's chin with his hand. "It's Young Macintosh, isn't it?"

Merida froze. Dad *did* know! But how?

"As the princess, you feel a responsibility to

help Young Macintosh," Fergus continued.

"But, Dad," Merida mumbled, "I *am* respon—"

Fergus pressed a finger to Merida's lips. "Hush. I'm happy to see you taking your role as princess so seriously. But your mother and I are working on a way to cure Young Macintosh. Now, if you really want to help, please find your brothers and make sure they haven't destroyed the whole festival."

Merida sighed, then went to find her brothers.

Out on the games field, Merida drifted through the hustle and bustle of the festival. She was surprised to see the triplets sitting quietly at a table.

When she tiptoed closer, she got a shock. The boys were playing *chess*. With Young Macintosh!

The triplets stared intently at the board. Then Hamish pointed at a piece. Hubert nodded in agreement. So Harris made their move.

"What?" Young Macintosh yelped. He frowned at the board. "Did you . . . Is that . . . checkmate?"

The boys grinned and nodded. Young Macintosh stood. He glared. And then the tantrum started.

"I can't lose to three wee babes! *Noooo!*" he sputtered, facedown on the ground. "How could I lose?" He kicked the table.

Merida chuckled. *Clearly he's still himself in some ways,* she thought. She was about to walk away when she saw something odd.

Even though Young Macintosh was still lying on the ground, he had raised his head enough to

peer at the triplets. And he was grinning! *What happened to the tantrum?* Merida thought. When Young Macintosh winked, the boys giggled with glee. And Merida was speechless.

He was faking it! Maybe he had even let the boys win. But why would he do that?

She glanced over at her brothers again. She'd rarely seen them so happy. *I'll bet the boys feel proud to have beaten someone so much older at a game like chess.* Maybe Young Macintosh had faked the tantrum to make the boys feel even better about their win.

Merida thought back to the tantrums she'd seen Young Macintosh throw. And she realized that a lot of the time, they happened after he'd lost at something that he really should have won.

Like losing at chess to three wee lads.

Could he have been losing on purpose? To make other people feel good?

It was a lot to think about. Ever since Young Macintosh had forgotten who he was, Merida was learning things about that she never knew. *He's funny and thoughtful,* she thought. *He doesn't like haggis!* She liked what she was learning.

Merida continued to walk around the festival. Scores of people were there now. Some were weaving straw into baskets. Others were leading their cows between the bonfires to protect them from fairies for the coming months. Tables all around showcased wares that people were hoping to sell.

Merida came across a tent filled with wood carvings. She picked one up and examined it. *These look familiar,* she thought.

A voice said, "Welcome to the Crafty Carver! I'm just back from the Stoneleigh festival, so I have all new stock. Holler if you see anything you like. Everything is half off."

Merida's head snapped up at the voice she heard. It was a voice she recognized—and one she would never forget. "It's you!" she sputtered. "You're the Witch!"

The old woman behind the table shook her head. "I'm just a humble wood-carver."

"No," said Merida, "you're the googly old witch who gave me that gammy spell that"— she stopped and looked around to make sure that no one else could hear—"that turned my mother into a bear!" she whispered. "That's even the same crow behind you!" At that, the crow squawked anxiously.

"I'm a wood-carver!" the woman answered.

"Witch!" Merida hissed.

"Wood-carver!"

Merida's head hurt from frustration. "Do we have to do this every time?"

The woman and the crow looked at each other. "Well . . . not every time!" the crow squawked.

The woman shrugged. "Fine, then. Not just a wood-carver."

Merida sighed. "I need your help. But I don't need a spell. I need something to break a spell."

The Witch raised an eyebrow. "And what will I get in exchange for my help?"

"Ach! What do you want? I can go back to the castle and get some money."

The Witch shook her head. "No. Not money.

I want an endorsement." She pulled out a sign that said THE CRAFTY CARVER. "I want you to write PRINCESS MERIDA'S FAVORITE WOOD-CARVER on this sign." She held out a quill.

Merida snatched the quill and scribbled on the sign. "There. Now can you help me?"

The Witch tucked the sign away. "So," she said, "what happened?"

Merida took a deep breath. "I'm not sure. But I think a fairy heard me make a careless wish."

"What did you wish for?"

"I wished that . . . that Young Macintosh would forget who he was."

The Witch gasped. "Jings crivens help ma boab! And a fairy heard that?"

Merida nodded.

"That's serious indeed!"

Chapter
6

The Witch gestured for Merida to duck behind her tablecloth.

"That's too small!" Merida protested.

"Huh!" the Witch snorted. "Too small!" She lifted the edge of the tablecloth and motioned again for Merida to come closer.

Reluctantly, Merida joined the Witch under

the table. But it was not the tiny, dark space she was expecting. In fact, the space under the table looked as large and spacious as any room in Castle DunBroch.

While Merida gaped, the Witch rummaged through a small bag. "Now, where did I put my . . ." She reached inside and pulled out a broom. "No, that's not it." Next out was a horn of some sort. "That's won't help, either."

"What are you looking for?" Merida asked.

The Witch was practically standing on her head inside the bag. Suddenly, she shouted, "Here it is!" She sprang back to her feet, holding a large cauldron. She staggered for a moment, and then dropped it in front of her.

"That *thing*," Merida said, "fit inside *that* bag?"

"This *room* fit under *that* table." The Witch

chuckled. "So why not? But there's no time for that, lassie. We need to get to work." She snapped her fingers and a fire appeared under the cauldron. Another snap and the cauldron filled with a bubbling liquid.

Then the Witch reached into the bag again. "Reversing a fairy's spell isn't easy," she muttered. She took out a scroll and handed Merida one end. "Here, lass, help me with this."

The Witch unrolled her end of the scroll and scanned the paper. "This won't help," she mumbled. "This is for a brownie infestation. . . . How about this one? No, that's a remedy for boggart bites. . . . Michty me! Look at this!"

"Michty me! Michty me!" the crow squawked.

"Did you find the remedy?" Merida asked.

"No, I found my granny's apple-blueberry tart recipe! I thought this was lost forever!"

Merida sighed. "Can you please look for the way to break the fairy spell?"

"Yes, yes," the Witch snapped. She went back to unrolling and reading the scroll. Soon the paper pooled around Merida's feet in waves.

Finally, the Witch shouted, "Aha! Here it is!"

"What does it say?" Merida asked.

"Let me see. . . . Reversing a fairy spell . . . It says you need to brew a tea of oak leaves, mistletoe, and the fingernails of black dog, and have the victim drink it."

Merida grimaced. "That's disgusting!"

"Oh, wait!" the Witch said. "That's only for breaking love spells."

"That's not what I need!" Merida groaned. "Maybe this was a bad idea."

Then the Witch shouted, "Here it is! This is the right one!"

"Are you sure this time?" Merida muttered.

The Witch scowled. "Yes, I'm sure. Do you want my help or not?"

Merida groaned again. "I do."

The Witch gave her a long look. "It says to reverse *any* fairy spell, the victim must stand on earth, be surrounded by clouds, and bathe in water—all at once."

Merida scratched her head. "What does that mean? Where could there be earth, clouds, and water all in the same place?"

The Witch shrugged. So did the crow.

"One more thing," the Witch added. "It also says that by the second sunrise, the spell will be permanent. So you'd better find that earth-cloud-water place soon, lassie."

Merida remembered when the Witch's spell had turned Mum into a bear that the spell needed to be broken by the second sunrise as well. "Is that second sunrise thing just standard language for magic?" she grumbled.

"Poetic, isn't it?" The Witch grinned.

Merida took a deep breath and covered her face with her hands. "I asked you to tell me how to break the spell," she said, "but what you told me doesn't help at all! I still have to figure it out!" She threw up her hands in frustration, but the Witch simply shrugged again.

Merida started to walk away, then stopped. "Why did you need the cauldron?"

"Oh, that," the Witch answered. "I was hungry. I thought I'd have some soup."

As Merida left the Witch, her stomach rumbled. She wished she'd taken a bowl of that soup. She shook her head and tried to focus on what the Witch had said. *The victim must stand on earth, be surrounded by clouds, and bathe in water—all at once.*

"Why does it always have to be a riddle?" she muttered. When she glanced back, the tent was gone. Merida sighed.

Then someone shouted, "Princess Merida!" It was Maudie, carrying a tray overflowing with food. "The banquet has begun, Princess. You should go join your parents."

"Thank you, Maudie," she said, taking two plates off the tray. On the dais, people had already started to eat. Elinor and Fergus did their best to be merry. But even from a

distance, Merida could see it wasn't going so well. Everyone at the table wearing Macintosh colors was either frowning or fretting. Young Macintosh himself, however, was nowhere to be seen.

Merida took her seat next to Elinor, preoccupied by what the Witch had told her.

"Merida?" said Mum. "Did you hear me?"

"Huh?"

"I asked you to pass the kippers to your father."

Merida grabbed the platter and passed it.

"Ach," Fergus said, "there's so much left! The last time we had a feast, Macintosh, your boy ate most all of the kip—" Fergus froze. "I'm...I'm sorry...," he stammered. But Lord Macintosh looked away.

Merida sighed. Just yesterday, Lord Macintosh had been bragging about how his son would climb the Crone's Tooth. And now . . .

Wait a minute! Merida thought. *The Crone's Tooth! That's it!* The place where someone could stand on earth, be surrounded by clouds, and bathe in water.

Young Macintosh just needed to bathe in the waters of the Fire Falls to get his memory back!

But almost immediately, Merida's shoulders slumped. How was she going to get him to the top of the Crone's Tooth?

Chapter 7

During every banquet meal she'd ever attended, Merida had wanted to get away. But today she had a real reason to leave. The sooner she found Young Macintosh, the sooner she could get him to the top of the Crone's Tooth. And the sooner she could fix everything she'd guddled.

But the meal had only just begun. And there'd be at least seventeen courses.

Merida tapped Mum's shoulder. "I've got dreadful collywobbles," Merida whispered. "I think I need to go lie down."

"Oh, lass!" Elinor cried. "Of course you should rest. But first have some haggis. Haggis always settles my stomach."

Now Merida's stomach truly did hurt.

Maudie set a plate down in front of Merida. She gulped. There was no way she could eat that and then climb the Crone's Tooth. She pushed the plate away.

"Merida?" Mum said. "Why aren't you eating?"

Merida bit her lip. The first plan didn't work. Maybe it was finally time to tell her mother the truth. Or at least some part of the truth.

"Mum," she whispered, "remember how you said that the princess has responsibilities?"

"Of course, lass, but what does that have to do with a bellyache?"

"There is something I need to do. May I be excused?"

Elinor raised an eyebrow. "What is it that you need to do? And does it have anything to do with Young Macintosh's lost memory?"

Merida opened her mouth to tell Elinor everything. But the conversation had gotten Fergus's attention. "What's going on?" he bellowed.

Now everyone at the table was looking at Merida—including Lord Macintosh. She couldn't just announce to everyone that she

had a plan to get Young Macintosh's memory back—because what if it didn't work?

She needed to look for Young Macintosh without everyone knowing. She looked at Elinor and whispered, "It's important, Mum. Can you please just trust me?"

Elinor tilted her head, then patted Merida's arm. "Our daughter is feeling unwell, Fergus. She needs to go and take care of that." Elinor turned back to Merida. "I trust all will be better when I see you next?"

Merida let out a deep breath. Then she reached for her mother's hand and squeezed it. "Thank you, Mum," she whispered. "Thank you for trusting me."

"I always will," Elinor answered.

As soon as Merida was out of sight of the guests, she changed course to search for Young Macintosh.

She found him sitting alone under a tree at the edge of the games field, fiddling with the petals of a wildflower. It was hard to recognize

him at first without his blue paint. But when he tossed his hair, the gesture was so familiar that Merida instantly knew it was him.

"Hello," Merida called. "I've been looking for you, Young Macintosh."

As soon as she spoke, the boy dropped the flower. "Are you talking to me?" he asked.

"W-well, yes," Merida stammered. "I came all the way here to find you."

"Are you going to try to fix me?" Young Macintosh asked.

Merida raised an eyebrow. "Fix you?"

Young Macintosh sighed. "All day long, one person after another has been trying to 'fix' my memory. I had to drink a foul-smelling tea that I swear had fingernail clippings in it. I've had a weird paste of cornmeal and something else applied to my forehead. Your father insisted that I must have lost my memory by getting hit in the head, so another hit would cure me. And then he hit me!"

Merida knew she shouldn't laugh, but a giggle escaped anyway. Young Macintosh glared—but only for a moment. Then he giggled, too.

"It didn't feel funny at the time," he said, "but I suppose it is a little funny."

Merida, laughing in earnest now, nodded.

When their laughter died down, Young Macintosh said, "I'm so sick of all these remedies. I can't listen to one more person's cure! So as long as you are not trying to fix me," he said, "would you like to sit?"

Merida sat and picked up the wildflower Young Macintosh had dropped. Now she played with its petals. How would she convince him to try *her* remedy when he was so sick of cures?

Young Macintosh interrupted her thoughts. "Why were you looking for me?"

Merida sighed. She'd have to try to break the spell without seeming like she was trying to get Young Macintosh's memory back. "I was hoping you would come with me to climb to the top of the Crone's Tooth. That was your plan, you know."

Young Macintosh shrugged. "Maybe. But I don't remember why it was important. So I don't really think I need to do it anymore."

Merida's fingers started to clench. But Mum had always said that one could catch more flies with honey. So she forced herself to smile and ask sweetly, "Won't you do it for me, Young Macintosh? Please?"

The boy's eyes narrowed as he stared at Merida intently. He was quiet for so long, her smiled began to crack. Finally, he said, "Are we friends?"

"Wh-what?" Merida stammered.

"Are we friends?" he asked. "Why would I do anything for you unless we are friends?"

Merida quickly turned away, pretending to look at a patch of clover. She didn't want Young Macintosh to see her face. Because she'd suddenly realized something awful.

Merida had practically grown up with Young Macintosh. She'd seen him at scores of banquets, festivals, and gatherings. Yet she couldn't remember ever speaking to him, other than to say hello.

In all those years, Merida hadn't made any effort to be Young Macintosh's friend.

Merida exhaled deeply. Then she turned to Young Macintosh. "I know you don't remember much," she said, "so I could tell you anything right now. But I don't want to lie to you." She bit her lip, suddenly nervous. "We're not friends. We've never been friends. And that's my fault. I'm the princess, and it was my responsibility to make you feel welcome." She paused and stared at the clover patch again. "Even though we haven't been friends in the past, I would like to get to know you now."

She stopped speaking, but Young Macintosh didn't say anything. In fact, the silence seemed to stretch for ages. Finally, Merida couldn't take it anymore. She looked at Young Macintosh, ready to convince him some more.

To her surprise, he was grinning at her. Merida noticed that without the blue woad, and with a smile, he looked a lot younger and far less fierce. "I know you have told me that my name is Young Macintosh, but it still doesn't feel right to me."

"Then what should I call you?"

"I think . . . ," he started, then took a deep breath. "I think I remember my friends calling me Ryan."

Now it was Merida's turn to grin. "Well then, Ryan," she said, "would you like to go for a ride through the countryside? It would be nice to talk."

Chapter 8

After saddling their horses, the two made their way into the Highlands. "You may have forgotten a lot of things," Merida said, "but riding isn't one of them!"

Ryan chuckled. "Some things come naturally, I guess."

When they came upon a long stretch of

straight road, Merida got an idea. "Do you want to test your skills?" she asked. "Care to race to that tree?"

"If you want us to be friends," Ryan said with a smile, "I'm not sure that my beating you will help that."

Merida laughed. "Let's just see who wins!" Soon the wind was whistling through her hair. Angus was fast, and Merida was an accomplished rider. But Ryan was even faster. He passed Merida and Angus, and no matter how she tried, Merida couldn't catch up.

The tree was in sight, and Ryan was still a whole length ahead of Merida. The road curved slightly—not enough to need to slow down. But when Ryan reached the curve, he slowed his horse. As soon as he did, Angus and Merida

raced past them to take the lead.

Merida reached the tree and turned to Ryan. He had jumped out of the saddle and was throwing one of his signature fits.

"Noooo!" he cried. He lay facedown, beating the ground with his fists.

Merida crossed her arms. "You can stop that, you big galoot. I know you let me win."

Ryan raised his head slightly, looking at Merida out of one eye. When she smiled, he stood and dusted himself off. "I thought it was the friendly thing to do," he said.

Merida smiled even harder.

Ryan reached into his saddlebag to get some carrots for his horse, and for Angus, too. It was another nice gesture that Merida had never seen him make before.

"It was friendly, I suppose," Merida said, "and I like to win—but only if it's fair and square."

Ryan nodded. "That's reasonable." He leaped into the saddle. "We should go again, then?"

Merida grinned and mounted Angus. The race began. They started neck and neck, but that only lasted for a moment. Ryan was soon far ahead of Merida. "Come on, Angus!" Merida urged. But the gap seemed too far to close.

Suddenly, Merida saw the familiar blue flickers that meant will o' the wisps were nearby. The wisps spooked Ryan's horse, and he threw Ryan—right into a pond.

Merida couldn't help laughing. "Who's going to win now?" she shouted as she approached Ryan, sputtering in the pond water.

But Angus clearly didn't think her taunt was

funny. When they reached the pond, he bucked and threw Merida into the water, too.

SPLASH!

Though she was dripping wet, Merida didn't want to get out of the pond. She couldn't remember the last time she'd laughed that hard.

Finally, Ryan stood and bowed to Merida. He looked ridiculous dripping mud and water.

"My lady," he said formally, "may I help you?"

Merida giggled, but she played along. "Yes, kind sir," she said.

Out of the corner of her eye, Merida spied wisps dancing around them. But at that moment, she was having too much fun to worry about fate.

"Now that we've bathed in pond water," Merida said, "are you ready to climb the Crone's Tooth?"

"Yes," Ryan said. Merida's face lit up. Then he added, "But first I want to go back to DunBroch and get something to eat. I missed the meal, you know. I'm starving!"

"Ach!" Merida groaned. She hated to waste any more time. But she didn't know how to make Ryan go with her to the Crone's Tooth.

Seeing her disappointment, Ryan said, "After we eat, we can climb, all right?"

There was nothing to be done, so Merida agreed. They rode quickly back to the games field, with Ryan chattering on about scones and mutton pies.

When they arrived, though, Merida knew that something was wrong. Fergus was wringing his hands, looking very worried, while Elinor spoke to Lord Macintosh. The Macintosh men were assembled. They looked ready to depart.

"Lord Macintosh," Elinor pleaded, "there's no reason to leave like this. I know you're upset about your son. We are, too! But give him some time to try to remember!"

"What's going on?" Merida asked.

"Oh," Elinor said, "Merida! Young Macintosh! You're back. We were just discussing—"

"NO!" Lord Macintosh roared. "I'm taking

my son, and we are returning to our lands." He grabbed Ryan's wrist. "Come on, son."

Ryan yanked away. "Wait one moment," he said. "I'm not going anywhere with this *stranger.*"

Lord Macintosh stiffened. He turned to his men and said coldly, "My son is leaving with us. If he won't go willingly, take him by force." He mounted his horse.

The men moved toward Ryan.

"Lord Macintosh," Elinor cried, "think about

what you're doing! You're scaring the boy." But Lord Macintosh didn't even acknowledge her.

One man tried to seize Ryan's arm. Ryan threw a punch. "Stay away from me!" he shouted.

Now more men approached Ryan, this time with swords drawn.

Fergus tried to ease the tension. "Everybody, just hold on. No need for swords or fighting. Let's just reason with the lad."

"No!" Lord Macintosh roared. "I am not waiting any longer! Get my boy!"

If Lord Macintosh takes Ryan away now, Merida thought, *I'll never get him to the Fire Falls—and he'll never get his memory back!*

She needed a distraction, something to allow her to get Ryan away from there. *But what?*

Chapter 9

Merida was on the verge of panic. She didn't know how to get Ryan away from the games field and to the Crone's Tooth. Then she saw the Witch sitting at her table, crow perched on her shoulder, trying to pretend she didn't notice the ruckus.

Merida ran over to her. "I need your help!"

"I'm just a humble wood-carver," the Witch answered.

Merida leaned over the table and grabbed the Witch's arm. "Listen, I've had enough of your jiggery-pokery. I'm a princess. You're a witch. That's just how it is." She looked over her shoulder. Armed men surrounded Ryan. She turned back to the Witch. "Now I need you to use your magic to make a distraction so I can get Ryan to the Fire Falls and break the fairy spell."

The Witch shrugged Merida's hands off. "Now, you listen to me, lassie! I don't have to do anything for anybody!"

"Please!" Merida pleaded. "I'll pay you!"

The Witch crossed her arms. "Not interested."

Merida clenched her teeth. Why couldn't

anything be easy? She didn't have time to argue with the woman. She needed help, and she needed it *now*.

Suddenly, she had an idea. She took a step back and muttered, "I bet you couldn't actually do it anyway."

"What?" the Witch hissed.

"Your magic probably isn't powerful enough to create a big enough distraction."

The Witch stammered, "I'll—I'll have you know . . . th-that . . . that—"

Merida cut her off. "Where are the triplets? They can handle this."

"Just you wait!" the Witch said. She took a small twig out of her pocket and, before Merida knew it, shouts came from the crowd.

Merida turned to see what had caused

the commotion. One of the unlit bonfires had suddenly come to life.

"What happened?" someone wailed.

"Is it fairy magic?" someone else shouted.

"Fairy magic," the Witch muttered. Then she pointed the twig at the other unlit bonfire. And just as suddenly, the first bonfire died down and the second one came to life.

Now the entire crowd—including Elinor,

Fergus, Lord Macintosh, Ryan, and all the Macintosh men—was entranced by the fires. Only the Witch didn't watch. She was discreetly pointing the twig this way and that. Wherever she pointed, a new fire was lit.

Merida quietly made her way through the crowd to get to Ryan. She seized his hand and pulled him behind a tent. "What are you doing?" he whispered.

She put a finger to her lips. She knew the distraction wouldn't last. She whispered back, "Do you trust me?"

"What?"

"I know we weren't friends before, but we are now. And if you can trust me, I think I can get your memory back."

"I don't know, Merida," he said, shaking his

head, "I'm not sure I can take any more cures."

"I know," Merida said, "but everyone else has been trying stupid things. I promise, if anything will work, this will."

Young Macintosh was about to shake his head again. So Merida blurted, "You don't realize what you've lost because you can't remember who you are. But who you are is someone special, someone worth remembering. Please let me show you that it's true."

Ryan stared at her for a long moment, then nodded. "Let's go."

Merida and Ryan rode as quickly as they could to the Crone's Tooth. Merida kept looking back to see if anyone was following. She couldn't yet see Lord Macintosh's men behind them, but she knew they would soon be on their heels.

As they rode, Ryan asked, "Are you going to explain what we're doing?"

"I think I know what happened to you," Merida said. "I think a fairy overheard something I said. We were arguing, you see, and . . . and I said something stupid."

"What?"

Merida sighed. "I wished for you to forget who you are." She hung her head. "I think a fairy heard my stupid wish and granted it to make mischief. I'm so sorry."

Ryan rode in silence for a moment, staring straight ahead. "So everything that has happened to me is because of you?"

Merida gulped and nodded. "Now the only way to break this spell is for you to bathe in the waters of the Fire Falls. But we have to do it by the light of the Spring Festival moon. So we have to climb the Crone's Tooth *tonight!*"

Ryan looked at her, silent again. Merida wasn't sure what he would do. Finally, he said, "Remind me when this is all over that you owe me big. I definitely don't want to forget that." He winked, and Merida knew he wasn't angry.

Ryan spurred his horse on. "Come on, Princess—we're in a hurry!"

When they arrived, the moon had begun to rise. Merida started scrambling up the rock.

But Ryan stood motionless, still on the ground.

"Why aren't you climbing?" Merida shouted.

Ryan stared up at the summit. "I think I remember being afraid of heights."

"But you're not! Just yesterday, we were racing up this rock!"

Ryan scratched his head. "I don't remember that. And I don't remember how to climb."

Merida heard distant hoofbeats now. They had to get to the Fire Falls before the soldiers arrived. She held out her hand. "I can help you climb. I promise I will get you to the top."

After a moment, he took her hand. She pulled him up the side of the rock that she knew was best. Together they began to climb. Merida told Ryan where to step and which outcrops to grasp on to. It wasn't easy, but slowly, they made their way up to the top.

Suddenly, someone shouted. "There they are!"

Ryan turned, but Merida cried, "Don't look down!" They were so close to the summit. She needed him to focus on going up, not on how far down the ground was.

The next voice, though, made Merida stop.

"Merida!" Elinor shouted. "This is no time for jiggery-pokery. Come down here at once!"

"I can't!" Merida called back. "Please, Mum, just give us a little time!"

"I've had enough of this!" Lord Macintosh bellowed. He looked at his men. "You three— climb up and get my son! If they won't come down, we will *bring* them down!"

Merida hoisted herself up to the summit of the Crone's Tooth. Then she leaned down to

offer Ryan a hand. As she raised him up, she said, "It's now or never."

The view from high atop the Crone's Tooth, lit by the moon, was breathtaking. But Merida barely glanced at anything except the waters of the Fire Falls.

Glittering behind the water, Merida spied a shimmering blue light. "A wisp!" she gasped. "We're on the right track!"

She gestured for Ryan to get under the flowing water. But he shook his head.

"Ummm," he mumbled, "I really don't want to get into that water."

Chapter 10

After everything they'd gone through, Merida couldn't believe it.

"But you have to!" she said.

"That water is freezing!"

"Ryan," Merida said through gritted teeth. "You need to stand on the summit of the Crone's Tooth, surrounded by clouds, and bathe in the waters of the Fire Falls in order to break the fairy spell." She pointed to the waterfall. "So get in. Now!"

Ryan took a step back. "Can I just put a hand under the water? Or just a foot?"

"Ryan!" Merida shouted. "I don't care about the cold. You have to do this!"

Ryan crossed his arms. "I don't think friends order each other around. And I really don't think this is going to work any better than the fingernail tea and getting hit in the head. So, if you don't mind, I'm going to skip the ice bath."

Why would he pick now to be a stubborn oaf? Merida thought. She glanced down and gulped. The Macintosh men had almost reached the summit. There wasn't much time.

There was only one thing left to do.

"Will you promise me something?" she asked.

Ryan uncrossed his arms. "Of course."

Merida put her hands on Ryan's arms. "No matter what happens," she said, "will you remember that we truly are friends?"

Before he could answer, Merida pushed him into the Fire Falls with her all her might.

In a moment, Ryan was soaked. He sputtered and struggled to stand.

Merida held her breath. *Please let this bring back his memory,* she thought.

Ryan wiped water from his face. "I can't believe you just did that!" he cried. "Who do you think you are?"

Merida felt tears welling in her eyes. It didn't work! Ryan still didn't remember anything. The disappointment was so strong, it felt

like someone had punched her.

Behind her, the Macintosh men neared the top of the mountain. She had to let them take Ryan now. Merida turned her face away so they wouldn't see her cry. She whispered, "I wish I'd never said those things."

"Hee-hee-hee."

Merida's head snapped up. "Did you hear that?" she said. "The giggling?"

She turned to face Ryan, who was no longer glaring. Instead he looked confused.

"Who do you think you are?" he repeated, though it was only a murmur now. Then he gasped. "You are . . . you are . . . the princess!"

He looked mortified. "I'm so sorry, Princess Merida. I can't believe I was yelling at you. . . ."

But Merida wasn't listening. She wrapped her arms around him, even though he was still dripping water. "You remember!" she shouted.

Merida was so thrilled, she almost forgot they were being chased. But the voices of the Macintosh men as they struggled to climb the last few meters of the Crone's Tooth brought her back to reality. "We'd better get down there," she said.

Ryan nodded. "I remember my father's temper. We don't want to face that!"

"So you remember everything?" Merida asked nervously.

He nodded again. "My name, my clan, my favorite food ... I even remember how you beat me three times—here at the Crone's Tooth, at our horse race, *and* at the Highland Games!"

Merida smiled. "I'm sorry about that—"

But Ryan cut her off. "Don't worry, Princess. I'll get you next time!"

Merida laughed and then leaned over the edge of the mountain. "We're coming down!" she called. "Right now!"

"Just be careful!" Elinor called back, cringing as she looked up. "It doesn't look safe!"

Merida began scrambling down the Crone's Tooth, with Ryan following. Every so often, her mother gasped. But Fergus kept saying, "She's fine, Elinor. Our daughter can handle this."

When Merida finally reached the ground, Elinor rushed to hug her. "Never," she said, "never again are you to climb anything at all!"

"Maybe just never until the next time," Fergus whispered.

Merida went to Lord Macintosh. "My lord," she said formally, "your son has his memory back!"

Lord Macintosh opened his mouth, but nothing came out.

It was Fergus who asked, "What? What do you mean? What happened up there?"

Merida laughed. "Why don't we let Young Macintosh tell you?"

She turned, expecting Ryan to be behind her. But he was still climbing down the mountain. Merida giggled. *I beat him again!* she thought.

As soon as Ryan got to the ground, he grabbed Lord Macintosh in a bear hug and lifted him off the ground. "Father!" he shouted.

Lord Macintosh gasped. "You remember me, son?"

Ryan nodded. "I remember everything." He smiled at Merida. "All because of her."

Merida blushed. But she was smiling, too.

"With Princess Merida's help, I got my memory back," he continued. "And I was able to reach my goal—I climbed to the top of the Fire Falls and I drank the waters."

"Well done, lad!" Fergus cheered.

Ryan knelt in front of Elinor. "As you know, I had another goal as well—to bring my queen a Lady Flower, to show my loyalty." He reached into a pocket and showed Elinor the flower.

"You did it!" she cried, taking the stalk of delicate white blooms from his hand.

"That's why it took you so long to get down from the summit," Merida said. "You were looking for a Lady Flower!"

Ryan grinned. And then, to everyone's surprise, he rose and held something out to Merida. It was another Lady Flower!

"What is this?" Merida sputtered.

"Well," Ryan said, "the Lady Flower is a symbol of loyalty. I am loyal to my queen. But I am also loyal to my *friend*."

Merida was speechless. Elinor said to Ryan, "You have honored Clan Macintosh today. We are all proud of you."

Fergus turned to Lord Macintosh and said, "I believe this calls for a toast!"

"Aye!" Lord Macintosh agreed. "To my son! And to his friends!"

Everyone cheered. But Ryan help up his hand for silence. "If I remember correctly, today is my birthday, and I haven't celebrated at all! Could we get back to the festival now and fix that?"

"That's a wise lad," Fergus laughed.

Everyone mounted their horses. Ryan pulled up next to Merida. "One more race?" he asked.

"As long as you know that even on your birthday"—Merida laughed—"I'm not going to let you win!"